Story Time for Little Monsters

The Littlest Zombie's Story

Written by Rusty Fischer
Illustrated by Joel Cook

magic wagon

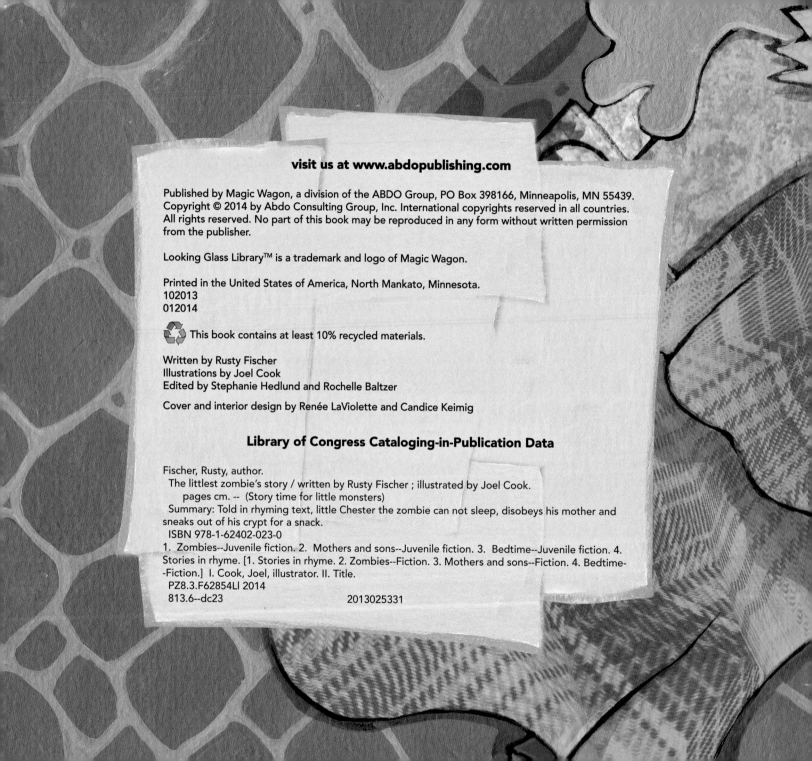

visit us at www.abdopublishing.com

Published by Magic Wagon, a division of the ABDO Group, PO Box 398166, Minneapolis, MN 55439.
Copyright © 2014 by Abdo Consulting Group, Inc. International copyrights reserved in all countries.
All rights reserved. No part of this book may be reproduced in any form without written permission
from the publisher.

Looking Glass Library™ is a trademark and logo of Magic Wagon.

Printed in the United States of America, North Mankato, Minnesota.
102013
012014

Written by Rusty Fischer
Illustrations by Joel Cook
Edited by Stephanie Hedlund and Rochelle Baltzer

Cover and interior design by Renée LaViolette and Candice Keimig

Library of Congress Cataloging-in-Publication Data

Fischer, Rusty, author.
 The littlest zombie's story / written by Rusty Fischer ; illustrated by Joel Cook.
    pages cm. -- (Story time for little monsters)
  Summary: Told in rhyming text, little Chester the zombie can not sleep, disobeys his mother and
sneaks out of his crypt for a snack.
  ISBN 978-1-62402-023-0
 1. Zombies--Juvenile fiction. 2. Mothers and sons--Juvenile fiction. 3. Bedtime--Juvenile fiction. 4.
Stories in rhyme. [1. Stories in rhyme. 2. Zombies--Fiction. 3. Mothers and sons--Fiction. 4. Bedtime-
-Fiction.] I. Cook, Joel, illustrator. II. Title.
  PZ8.3.F62854Ll 2014
  813.6--dc23   2013025331

Little Chester tossed and turned inside the crypt so dreary. If zombies could break down and cry, he would have gotten teary.

It was the darkest dead of night
inside the family crypt,
as into Chester's little tomb
his mother quietly slipped.

"What is wrong, oh little one?"
Chester's mom asked with a sigh.
"You look as if you've bitten
into a moldy piece of thigh."

"Now quiet down and hear my plea,"
poor Chester's mother cooed.
"You must learn to ease your mind
and think no more of food."

Poor Chester frowned and squirmed,
then said, "Good luck, oh Mother dear."
His mother said, "Now settle down
and lend your mom an ear . . ."

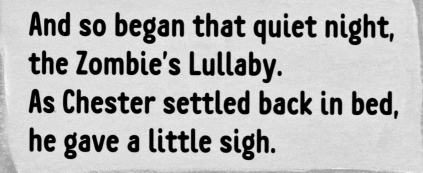

And so began that quiet night,
the Zombie's Lullaby.
As Chester settled back in bed,
he gave a little sigh.

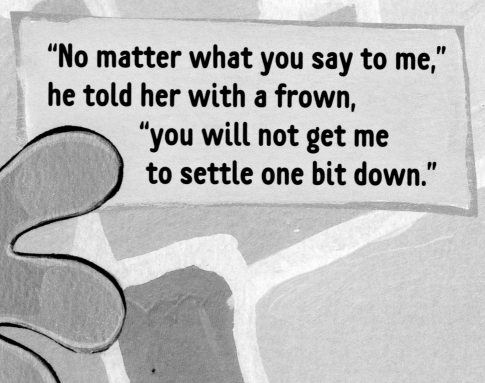

"No matter what you say to me,"
he told her with a frown,
"you will not get me
to settle one bit down."

"We'll see," she smiled
knowingly while holding
Chester's hand.
"For now, lie still and
close your eyes and
drift to la la land."

So Chester did as he was told
and snuggled into bed.
Chester's mother took a breath
then went on and said:

"For little ones who cannot sleep I croon this lullaby. You say you cannot sleep, my sweet? Well here, give this a try:

"When sleep is furthest from your mind, there's just one thing to do. First, you must count to number one and then to number two.

"'What will I count?' I hear you ask.
Well, here's what I suggest:
Count all the brains you've ever munched!
Yes, those you've liked the best.

"Count fingers, toes, and abdomens
you've chomped on with your teeth.
And soon, my little undead one,
you'll find such sweet relief . . ."

Chester's mom was winding down.
He saw her eyes grow bleary.
And then she yawned and yawned
again as her head grew oh so weary.

Chester smiled and moved aside
so his mother could lie down.
And as she sped to slumber land,
he looked down with a frown.

Yes, Chester's mom dozed off right quick.
Yet how he yearned to run.
He felt, in fact, more hungry now
than when her lullaby had begun!

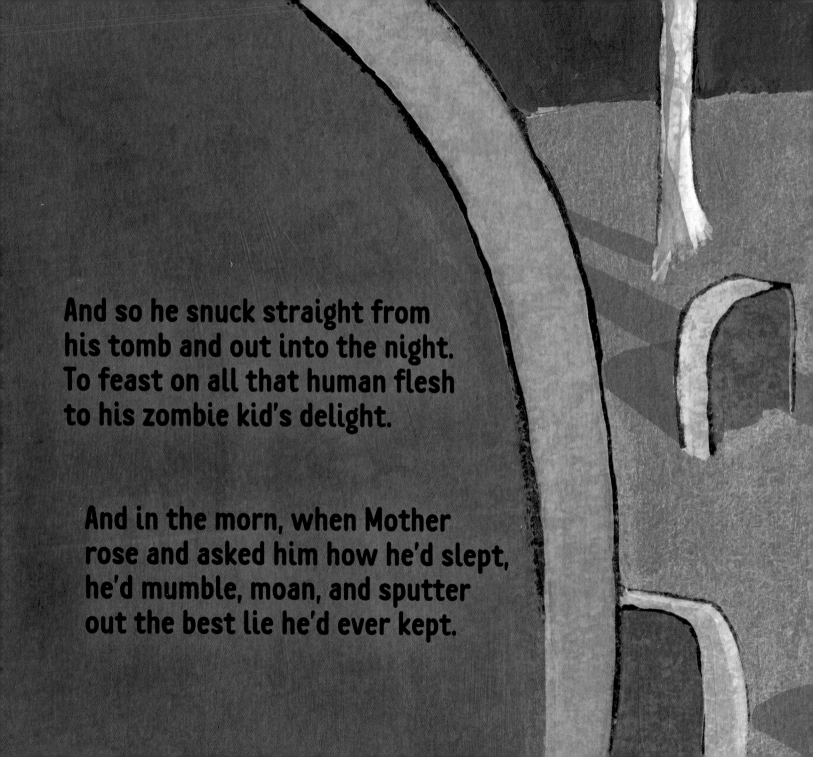

And so he snuck straight from
his tomb and out into the night.
To feast on all that human flesh
to his zombie kid's delight.

And in the morn, when Mother
rose and asked him how he'd slept,
he'd mumble, moan, and sputter
out the best lie he'd ever kept.